MORE CAPS FOR SALE

More Caps for Sale: Another Tale of Mischievous Monkeys
by Esphyr Slobodkina with Ann Marie Mulhearn Sayer
Production assistant & colorist Katherine Grace Larsen
Text copyright © 2015 by Ann Marie Mulhearn Sayer
Artwork copyright © 2015 by Ann Marie Mulhearn Sayer and Esphyr Slobodkina
For information address HarperCollins Children's Books, a division of HarperCollins
Publishers, 195 Broadway, New York, NY 10007.
www.harpercollinschildrens.com

ISBN 978-0-06-240545-6 (hardcover) — ISBN 978-0-06-249957-8 (pbk.)

The artist used a modern collage technique, using original art by Esphyr Slobodkina and
utilizing Photoshop, to create the digital illustrations for this book.
21 22 23 24 25 SCP 10 9 8 7 6 5 4 3 2

First Edition

MORE CAPS FOR SALE

Another Tale of Mischievous Monkeys

Esphyr Slobodkina

with
Ann Marie Mulhearn Sayer

HARPER

An Imprint of HarperCollinsPublishers

Once there was
a peddler who sold caps.
But he was not like
an ordinary peddler
carrying his wares on his back.
He carried them
on top of his head.

First he had on his own
checked cap,
then a bunch of gray caps,
then a bunch of brown caps,
then a bunch of blue caps,
and on the very top
a bunch of red caps.

While the peddler traveled home that day
he thought about
the bunch of monkeys
who had taken his caps.

It took so long to get them back,
he hadn't sold any caps,
not even a red cap.

As he walked along,
he did not look back.

He did not see the monkeys
come down from the tree.

He did not see them following him.

Right foot, left foot.

Right foot, left foot.

All in step.

When the peddler got home
he was very hungry,
but he could not eat.

He was worried.

He had not sold any caps.

Then he looked out the window.
And what do you think he saw?

There, in the tree
behind his house,
sat the monkeys
eating *their* supper.

Suddenly
the peddler
was hungry, too.
He reached for his bowl
and ate every drop.

After the peddler cleaned his plate,
he went out
and looked at the monkeys.

"You monkeys, you,"
he said, shaking his finger at them.
"You must go home."

But the monkeys
only shook their fingers
back at him and said,
"Tsz, tsz, tsz."

Then each monkey dropped a banana skin
down to the ground.

The peddler was so upset,
he could not speak.
He picked up a banana peel,
walked to the trash barrel,
and threw it away.

He went into the house,
slamming the door.

He did not see
each monkey
come down from the tree,
pick up a banana peel,
and throw it
in the trash barrel, too.

"Oh, those monkeys,"
the peddler thought.
"They have
followed me home,
made a mess
of my yard,
and today
I have sold no caps."

He walked up and down the hall.
He walked so much
that soon it was time
for bed.

But the peddler could not fall asleep.

He turned on his right side.
No sleep.

He turned on his left side.
No sleep.

He lay on his back.
No sleep.

Then he looked out the window into the tree.
And what do you think he saw?

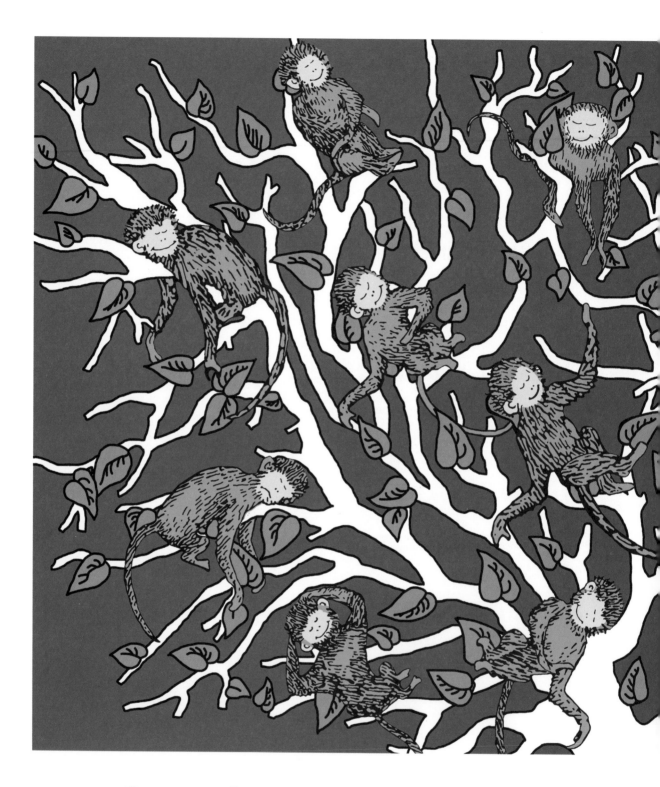

On every branch lay a monkey
falling asleep, so peacefully that

the peddler began feeling tired, too.

So he went to sleep.

When the peddler woke up,
he was refreshed and rested.

He jumped out of bed and began to dress.

He ate his breakfast
and was ready to go to work.

First he put on his own
checked cap,
then a bunch of gray caps,
then a bunch of brown caps,
then a bunch of blue caps,
and on the very top
a bunch of red caps.

He forgot all about the monkeys.

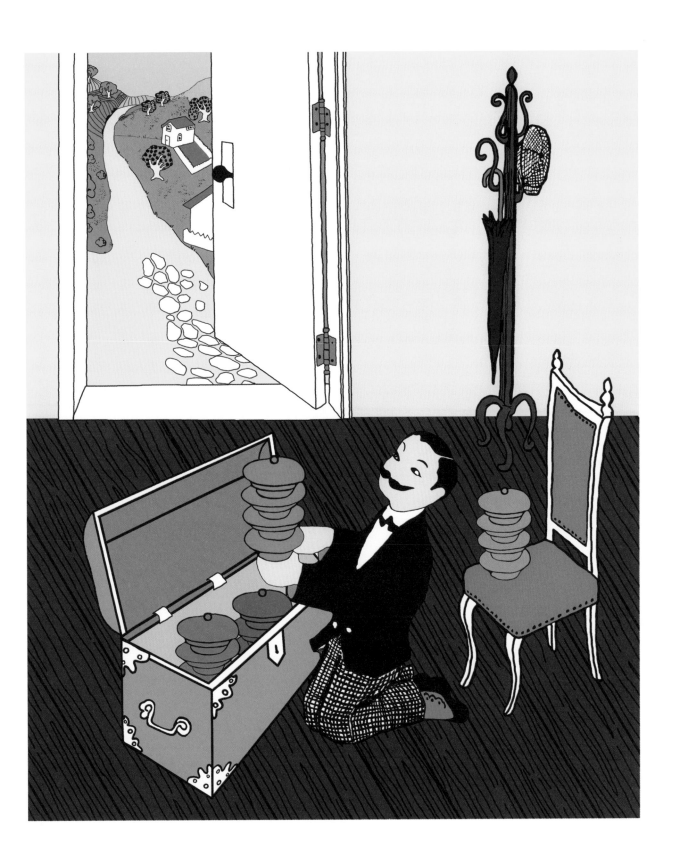

As he walked along,
he did not look back.

He did not see the monkeys
come down from the tree.

He did not see them following him.

Right foot, left foot.
Right foot, left foot.
All in step.

The town was busy.

Some people were going to work.

Some people were walking their dogs.

Some people were shopping.

Everyone passed by the peddler.
They watched him
point to the top of his head
and call,
"Caps! Caps for sale!
Fifty cents a cap!"

Then they watched the line of monkeys
behind him
point to their heads.

As the peddler sold a cap,
he bowed to say, "Thank you."
When the peddler bowed,
the monkeys bowed, too.

Everyone was smiling to see such a sight.

One by one the townspeople
began to buy the caps.

By the afternoon
the peddler had sold
all his caps.

When he got to the end of the town,
the peddler turned
to walk home.

And what do you think he saw?

All the monkeys lined up in a row.

"You monkeys, you,"
the peddler said,
shaking his finger at them.
"You must go home!"

But the monkeys
only shook their fingers
back at him and said,
"Tsz, tsz, tsz!"

The peddler gave up.
He was too tired
to argue
with the monkeys.

Besides, he was very happy.

Today he had sold all his caps—
the gray, the brown, the blue, and the red.

He slowly walked home,
remembering the day.

He did not see the monkeys
walking behind him.

Right foot, left foot.
Right foot, left foot.
All in step.

ABOUT THE AUTHORS

Ann Marie Mulhearn Sayer began an association with Esphyr Slobodkina in 1994. Although separated in age by over forty years, the women soon became fast friends.

Sayer and Slobodkina found they shared a synchronicity in thinking: an out-of-the-box approach to creative endeavors and problem solving. Sayer was originally hired to produce musical versions of Slobodkina's children's books, but she ultimately served as her personal assistant from January 1996 to July 2002. In 1998 Slobodkina asked Sayer if she would relocate from West Hartford, Connecticut, to Long Island and reside in an apartment above the main residence to facilitate their business venture. Sayer, who was finishing studies at the University of Hartford at the time, agreed to the arrangement. The two women worked continuously in those years, and twelve-hour days were nothing out of the ordinary. They attended many art exhibitions, where Slobodkina's work was on view, and theatrical programs, where Sayer performed the musical narrative production of *Caps for Sale.* In her late eighties and early nineties, Slobodkina spoke at many of the venues. Although abstract painting and assemblage art was her primary focus, she shared a common interest with Sayer in writing and storytelling.

Sayer scored musical versions for five of Slobodkina's children's books during Slobodkina's lifetime. Slobodkina painstakingly evaluated every motive and lyric, suggesting changes or elaborating on a character's intended temperament, giving Sayer a grasp of every personality in the stories.

Sayer and Slobodkina spent hours talking about children's books. In agreement that society bears a critical responsibility to instill morality and ethics in its young people during their formative years, both considered children's books a perfect conveyance for the task.

It was Slobodkina's wish that after her death, Sayer continue her work and keep Slobodkina's art, books, and illustrations in the public eye for future generations to enjoy. In the year 2000, Esphyr Slobodkina formed the Slobodkina Foundation. Ann Marie Mulhearn Sayer serves as president of the Slobodkina Foundation and has been administrating, cataloging, and exhibiting Slobodkina's fine art, children's books, textiles, and publications for over eighteen years. In 2010, Sayer concluded a three-year project producing a traveling exhibition of the largest collection of Esphyr Slobodkina's art. She then turned her eye to Slobodkina's children's books.

More Caps for Sale is based on story ideas from Slobodkina's and Sayer's imagination, with prior permission from Slobodkina. The story of *More Caps for Sale* is not only a continuation of *Caps for Sale* but also woven from concepts and motion present in Slobodkina's first illustrated children's book, *Mary and the Poodies* (unpublished). In *Mary and the Poodies*, Mary inadvertently learns good behavior by mimicking her imaginary friends, "the Poodies." In *More Caps for Sale*, the mindful monkeys watch the peddler and unintentionally learn proper conduct.

When Sayer finished the text for this sequel, she made a list of objects she would need for each page's illustration. Intimate knowledge of the subject matter in Slobodkina's paintings and illustrations supplied Sayer with a mental archive of source material from which to choose. She then scanned, extracted, and manipulated images to create the desired scenes. Every tree, chair, lamp, building, cap, and, of course, monkey was produced using Slobodkina's original art. Although many of the images were scanned from *Caps for Sale* illustrations, the peddler's bed and some of the people were extracted from *Circus Caps for Sale*, the house from *Jack and Jim*, the furniture from *Moving Day for the Middlemans*, and the banana from Slobodkina's oil painting *Still Life with Bananas*.

Reflecting upon hours of conversations with Slobodkina on perspective and her choices in stylization, Sayer employed great care to develop each layout as the artist herself might have done.